For Hannah and Jake — EEW
To the amazing Ellmann family — RB

Text copyright © 2003, 1995 by Ellen Emerson White.
Illustrations copyright © 2003 by Robert J. Blake.
All rights reserved. Published by Scholastic Inc. SCHOLASTIC, CARTWHEEL BOOKS,
and associated logos are trademarks and/or registered trademarks of Scholastic Inc.

Library of Congress Cataloging-in-Publication Data

White, Ellen Emerson.
Santa paws : the picture book / by Ellen Emerson White;
illustrated by Robert Blake.
p. cm.
"Cartwheel Books."
Summary: A dog living on the street struggles with cold weather
at Christmas time, becomes known for his good deeds,
and finally finds a home.

ISBN 0-439-32438-6

1. Dogs--Juvenile fiction. [1. Dogs--Fiction.
2. Christmas--Fiction.] I. Blake, Robert, ill. II. Title.
PZ10.3.W5843 San 2003   [E]--dc21   2002014127

10 9 8 7 6 5 4 3 2 1   03 04 05 06 07

Printed in Mexico 49
First printing, October 2003

Reinforced Binding for Library Use.

SANTA PAWS

By Ellen Emerson White
Illustrated by Robert J. Blake

SCHOLASTIC INC.

New York Toronto London Auckland Sydney Mexico City New Delhi Hong Kong Buenos Aires

It WAS ALMOST CHRISTMAS, AND THE DOG WAS ALONE. He lived by himself on the streets, so he had no warm place to sleep, and no food to eat. But, more than anything, he wanted to have a family of his very own to love. And, if he was lucky, maybe they would love him, too!

Today, the ground was covered with fresh snow, and the dog's paws were so cold that he could barely feel them. There was a trash can on the street corner, and he sniffed it eagerly. Doughnuts! And pizza crusts! Yay! He tipped the can over and had a late breakfast.

Feeling much better, he trotted up the sidewalk. It was probably time to take a nap now. Even though he always slept at night, he made sure to take several naps during the day, too. Naps were fun! Besides, it would be too sad to be lonely *and* tired. And the dog really didn't like being sad.

He dug himself a nice nest in the snow next to a big brick building. Then he curled up and went to sleep. He was snoring happily and dreaming about finding a whole bucket of hot fried chicken, when suddenly something hit him right on the head! Ow!

Alarmed, he jumped to his feet. What was it? He saw a large red rubber ball buried in the snow. Was the ball alive? Had it thumped his head on purpose? What a mean ball! Maybe he should bite it.

Two boys, Gregory and Oscar, ran over to get their lost ball, but then they stopped.

"Help!" Oscar shouted, and he flung himself to the ground. "It's a snow monster!"

"No, it's a dog," Gregory said.

Oscar grinned at him as he got back up. "No. Really, Greg?"

Gregory just laughed, and started brushing the snow off the dog's back and head.

Someone was patting him! Wow! The dog wagged his tail wildly. Had he found a new friend? A friend who would love him? Oh, that would be *so fun*.

"Do you think he's lost?" Gregory asked Oscar. "He doesn't have a collar."

"Maybe," Oscar said. "If you brought him home, would your parents let you keep him?"

"I don't know," Gregory said. "They might not want us to get another dog yet." His family's old collie, Marty, had died recently, and they all still missed him very much.

The dog wagged his tail and leaned against Gregory's leg. He liked this nice boy. He liked him very much.

Just then, a loud bell rang. The brick building was a middle school, and recess was over now.

Gregory patted the dog again. "Good boy. Go home now, okay?"

The dog watched miserably as his new friend walked away. His tail drooped, and he slumped down into the snow.

He was alone again.

The dog waited on the playground for a long time, but none of the children came back outside. He was so sad that he whimpered to himself a few times. Then he sighed.

It was time to be on his way.

Every day, the dog liked to walk around town and watch all of the nice people going here and there. The town was called Oceanport, and he thought it was very pretty.

He also liked to sniff the salty smell of the sea when he held his nose up into the wind.

It was just getting dark when he heard a small voice cry out in pain. He stopped in the middle of the street and held up one paw. What was wrong? Was someone in trouble?

He trotted over to a nearby house and found an elderly woman lying in the driveway. She had slipped on the ice and broken her hip. He woofed softly at her.

"Please help me," she whispered.

The dog raced back out to the street and looked in both directions. What should he do? Where should he go? He saw some people getting out of a car, and barked loudly at them. It was Mrs. Goldstein, and her three children, on their way home from the store.

"Harold, go see what that dog wants," she said to her youngest son, with her arms full of grocery bags.

The dog kept barking, and ran back and forth.

"I don't think I should," Harold said, and sniffled loudly. "I might be allergic."

"You're not allergic," his brother Brett said. "You're just a big baby."

"I am not!" Harold said, and sniffled again.

"Okay, okay, I'll go," their sister Lori said.

The dog led her over to the driveway where the injured woman was lying.

"Oh, no," Lori gasped. "Mom! Call an ambulance! Mrs. Amory fell down!"

As more neighbors ran outside to help, the dog moved into the shadows to hide.

"It was like the movies," Harold kept telling everyone. "The dog came, and we followed him, and it was really cool! He was a hero!"

"Did we follow the dog?" Lori asked Brett.

"Yes," Brett said with a grin. "But we brought lots of tissues with us, just in case."

Once the dog was sure that Mrs. Amory was safe, he started down the street.

It was time to be on his way again.

The dog spent the night alone in the woods. He found a little rock cave and snuggled up in a pile of dry leaves. His stomach hurt because he was hungry. But maybe tomorrow he would be able to find some food. He fell asleep, and dreamed about his new friend Gregory. He couldn't wait to see him again!

But, during the night, it began to snow. In fact, it was a blizzard! The wind howled so loudly that it made the dog's ears hurt.

When the snow finally stopped the next day, the dog galloped outside. Some of the snow was so deep that it was over his head! He had to keep leaping over the piles so that he wouldn't be buried. It was hard work!

The dog ran directly to the school playground to look for Gregory. But no one was there. So, the dog sat down to wait. He waited, and waited, and waited. To pass the time, he rolled over, dug a few holes in the snow, and scratched behind each of his ears. Then he yawned, and stretched, and started all over again.

Finally, he was so bored that he had to take a nap.

"You came back!" a voice said happily. "What a good dog."

Gregory! With his friend Oscar! The dog sprang to his feet. He wagged his tail and let them take turns patting him.

"Maybe I should ask my parents if I can have a dog for Christmas," Gregory said.

"You should cry when you do it," Oscar advised. "And make your voice shake, too."

"What are you doing over there, boys?" one of their teachers, Mrs. Hennessey, called. "Get away from that animal! He might be dangerous!"

"He's—my dog," Gregory said quickly. "He must have followed me here."

"What's his name?" Mrs. Hennessey asked with her hands on her hips.

"Sparky," Gregory said, just as Oscar said, "Rover."

Mrs. Hennessey frowned.

"Um, Rover is his middle name," Gregory said.

"Well, I don't like it when children fib," Mrs. Hennessey said sternly. "I want you two boys to go right down to the office and talk to the principal about this. Now, march!"

The dog stopped wagging his tail as Gregory and Oscar walked slowly back inside the school. Why did his new friend keep going away? It made him very sad.

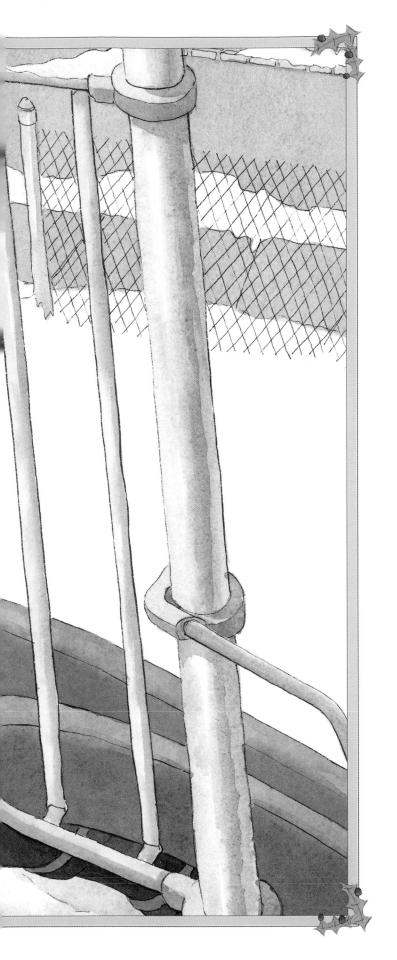

The dog waited for Gregory to return, but he never did. So the dog went back to sleep. This time, a different voice woke him up. It was Patricia, who was Gregory's big sister.

"Are you the dog my brother won't stop talking about?" she asked.

The dog waved his tail nervously. Was this girl his friend? It was hard to tell.

"He had to stay after school because of you," Patricia said. "So. Do you do any tricks?"

The dog cocked his head.

"Speak!" she said.

The dog lifted his paw.

"Okay," she said. "Lie down."

The dog raised both paws now, so that he was begging.

"You may be cute, but you are very silly," Patricia said. Then she reached into a brown paper bag and pulled out two chicken sandwiches. "Here, we saved our lunches for you. We'll bring more food tomorrow. Stay, okay? Stay."

The dog barked, and then rolled over twice.

Patricia laughed, and walked away.

The dog enjoyed the sandwiches very much. After that, he decided to take his usual long walk around town. He wandered all the way down to the park. Every year, during the holidays, the town set up a special exhibit called the Festival of Many Lands.

There were some big boys talking and laughing near the Nativity scene. They were knocking it over!

The dog tore across the park to stop them. What they were doing was wrong!

He growled and barked loudly at them until they ran away. Then he yawned. It was very late, and he was getting sleepy.

There was a large sleigh in the park, with a statue of Santa Claus, and eight plastic reindeer. The dog jumped up and landed right in Santa Claus's lap.

Then he climbed onto the blankets in the back of the sleigh. It was a perfect place to spend the night!

The next morning was a bright and sunny day. The dog gave himself a good morning "Woof" and then sat up in the front of the sleigh. It was fun to be so high off the ground.

A man walking by the park stopped and stared.

"Look," he said to his friends. "It's Santa Paws!"

They all laughed and waved at the dog.

Yay! They liked him! The dog wagged his tail and barked once. Then he sat back down to enjoy the sunshine.

After a while, he decided to go for a walk and look for food. He was trotting down a country lane when he saw something very strange. There were cows everywhere! Lots and lots of black and white cows mooing! Right in the middle of the road! In his way!

The dog looked at the cows, and the cows looked at the dog.

Then, the dog barked. To his surprise, the cows began to shuffle down the road. So he kept barking, and they kept moving. Then they began to run!

That made the dog nervous, so he raced in front of them and barked some more. The cows turned around and started to run in the other direction!

That seemed wrong, so the dog chased after them. He barked until they were going the right way again. That was much better.

He herded the cows down the road until they came to a long driveway. The cows all turned left and ambled up the driveway.

The dog followed them until they got to a big, wooden barn. He wasn't sure what to do next, so he just barked.

A skinny woman in a huge parka came out of the barn and stared. "Mortimer!" she bellowed. "The cows came home!"

Her husband wandered outside. "Weird," he said, and went back into the barn.

The dog barked once and trotted towards the main road.

He was late for school!

But when he got to the school, it was deserted. Where was Gregory? Would he ever come back? Oh, this was very, very bad.

He waited for several hours, but no one came.

Maybe he would go look for Gregory. He walked for miles, but the only people he saw were strangers. He cheered up a little when he found some leftover spaghetti and meatballs in a trash can. But as soon as he finished eating, he felt unhappy again.

Then the dog found himself in a huge empty parking lot near some low buildings.

He walked over to explore the buildings. When he stepped on a rubber mat, a pair of doors opened right in front of him. It was magic!

The dog decided to go inside. He had never seen a place like this. The lights were out, but there were stores everywhere. He could smell leftover food, too. Where was he?

He wandered around the dark mall until he finally found something familiar.

There was a big wooden sleigh, with eight plastic reindeer! The dog wagged his tail and jumped inside to go to sleep. What luck!

When he woke up, there were crowds of people shopping. So the dog crawled deeper into the sleigh and hoped that no one would see him. But then people began shouting "Where is he?" and "Has anyone seen a lost little boy?"

The dog poked his head over the edge of the sleigh. Why were they all so upset? Everyone was shouting and rushing around in a panic. What was wrong?

He thought he heard a tiny splash and a gurgle. He stood up, and then he sailed out of the sleigh with one great leap. He raced down the entire length of the mall and flung himself into a bubbling fountain. A small boy had fallen into the water, and he was drowning!

The dog dove underneath the water and used his teeth to pull the boy up to the surface. Then he did his best to bark and keep them both afloat at the same time.

The little boy's father ran over and lifted his son out of the fountain. The dog scrambled out and shook the water off his fur.

"Thank you," the man said gratefully. "You saved my son."

Everyone standing nearby began to clap. The dog didn't know if clapping was good or bad, so he ran for the exit.

.

By chance, Gregory had come to the mall with Patricia and his mother, Mrs. Callahan, to do some shopping. He was stunned when he saw the dog race past them and outside.

"Mom, look!" he said. "That's my dog!"

"Figures," Patricia said. "Someone must have told him to 'sit,' and he thought that meant that he should go shop."

Gregory ran as fast as he could, but when he got to the front door, all he could see was a crowded parking lot.

The dog was gone.

After that rescue, everyone in town began talking about Santa Paws. People wondered where he might appear next, and who he would save this time. Gregory and his family even watched a story about the dog on television! The newscasters showed an artist's sketch of Santa Paws, and asked anyone who saw him to call a special Santa Paws hotline. They described the dog as being small, and brown, and very, very wise.

The next day was Christmas Eve, and Mr. Callahan drove Gregory over to the school to leave some food for the dog. The family had decided that they wanted to keep Santa Paws — if they could find him! Gregory spent the entire afternoon at the playground, but the dog did not come back. When it was time for supper, Gregory gave up and let his father take him home.

In the meantime, the dog was sitting in a vacant lot, shivering. His fur had gotten wet when he jumped in the fountain. It was so cold outside that he was now covered with ice! His teeth were even chattering!

He started limping down the street, even though he didn't know where to go. He was too cold to think. He was even too cold to sleep. He just put one paw in front of the other and walked through the dark night.

Then, suddenly, he smelled smoke. He sniffed the air and then followed the scent to the house where the Brown family lived. They were all asleep in their bedrooms, and the dog barked and scratched at the door to try and wake them up. Their house was on fire!

So he took a running start and crashed right through the front window.

The living room was burning, and the air was thick with smoke. The dog ran up the stairs, barking loudly. He barked until the entire family was awake. Then he guided all of them safely outside.

By now, the fire trucks were arriving. The firefighters put out the fire with their hoses, and then the fire chief came over to talk to the family.

"Is everyone okay?" he asked.

"Yes, thank you," Mr. Brown said. "He saved us."

Fire Chief Jefferson looked puzzled. "Who saved you?"

"Who else?" the Browns said together. "It was Santa Paws!"

They all turned around to admire the hero dog, but he was nowhere in sight.

Once again, Santa Paws had left the scene.

The dog had burned his paws badly when he ran through the fire, and it hurt to walk. He had cut himself on glass, too. But he was so lonely and hungry that he just kept plodding from street to street. He hung his head and let his tail drag on the ground as he limped along.

It was Christmas morning, and there was a beautiful white building with a steeple up in front of him.

Every year, no matter what religion they were, everyone in town came together to celebrate the holiday season. This year, the ceremony was at the Catholic church, and the local rabbi was leading the service. He was giving a speech about the magic of a dog named Santa Paws, when the front doors creaked open.

The dog walked up the main aisle. Then, he staggered and collapsed onto the floor.

Gregory and his family were sitting near the front of the church.

"My poor dog," Gregory said. Then he ran down the aisle to greet him, while everyone else clapped and cheered.

When he saw Gregory, the dog lifted his head and began to wag his tail weakly.

Patricia stepped out into the aisle. "Is there a veterinarian in the house?" she asked.

Two people raised their hands and came over to examine Santa Paws. The dog wagged his tail, but kept his eyes on Gregory the entire time. Now that he had finally found his friend, he was not going to lose him again. Ever!

"Don't worry," one of them said to Gregory. "Your dog is going to be just fine."

Gregory looked up at his parents eagerly. "Is he really my dog now?"

Mr. and Mrs. Callahan nodded and smiled.

"Actually, he's *our* dog," Patricia said.

"Okay," Gregory said, and gave Santa Paws a big hug. "Merry Christmas, Santa Paws. Let's go home!"

Home? He had a home? A real home? And a new family who loved him? Yay! The dog barked and wagged his tail and barked some more.

It was the best Christmas ever!